An angel of my own!

Written by Beth Roberts

Illustrated by Caroline Jayne Church

PaRragon

Bath · New York · Singapore · Hong Kong · Cologne · Delhi · Melbourne

Lizzie was a pretty little girl
who lived with her mom,
her dad, and her baby
brother Matthew.
Lizzie had bright eyes,
chestnut-brown hair,
and rosy cheeks.
She looked as good and
sweet as a little angel,
although she didn't
always act like one.

Lizzie wasn't always good and sweet. In fact, sometimes she could be very, very naughty!

One day, Lizzie was naughtier than she'd ever been before.
In the morning, she decided to play with her toys. Lizzie got out all
of her dolls, and then she got out all of her crayons.
Next she got out her building blocks, and then she got out her tea set.

Soon, all of Lizzie's toys were out of the toy box
and spread all over the floor.
By lunchtime, Lizzie had made a bit of a mess.
"Please put away your toys now, Lizzie," said Mom.
"No!" Lizzie said. "I don't want to!"
So Mom had to put everything away all by herself.

That afternoon, Lizzie's grandma came to visit.
Grandma was very pleased to see Lizzie and baby Matthew.
"Lizzie, please give your grandma a kiss hello," said Mom.
But Lizzie ran away from Grandma into the yard.
She sat by herself for a while, before creeping
back to the house.

Lizzie peeked through the window and saw everyone enjoying some yummy treats without her. Lizzie wished she hadn't been so rude. If she said she was sorry she would be able to join the others, but she didn't do that because she was too busy sulking.

That night, as her mother tucked her into bed and kissed her good night, Lizzie felt unhappy. She thought about all the naughty things she'd done. Lizzie hadn't had a very good day, and now she wished she could make everything all right.
Soon Lizzie's eyes began to feel heavy, and a minute later she fell fast asleep.

In the middle of the night,
Lizzie was dreaming peacefully.
Suddenly a strange glow
filled the room. Lizzie opened
her eyes—and next to her bed
was a beautiful angel.
The angel had a kind face and
wonderful, shimmering wings.
She was glowing with a bright
golden light.

"Hello, Lizzie," smiled the angel.
"Don't be afraid. I know that you're
feeling a bit sad. I've come to try
to help you."

"You're very pretty," Lizzie
whispered. "Who are you?"
The angel smiled.
"I'm your friend," she replied.

The angel took Lizzie by the hand.
"Sit with me," the angel said.
"Let's talk about all the things
that happened today,
and think about how we
could have made them better.
Putting away toys isn't much fun, is it?"
Lizzie shook her head.

"But if you don't tidy up, people can hurt themselves falling over toys on the floor," said the angel.
Lizzie smiled. "I want to help Mom. I'll try to put my things away from now on," she said.

"It would make your grandma so happy if you would spend time with her. You could have a lot of fun together," continued the angel, "and think of all the delicious treats you can have together."
"I didn't mean to run away from Grandma," said Lizzie.

"And what about baby Matthew?"
asked the angel. "If you *do* accidentally
wake him up, why don't you try to make
him laugh instead of cry?"
Lizzie nodded her head happily.
That was a good idea. Lizzie felt
much better.

The angel tucked Lizzie back into bed and stroked her face tenderly.
"I wish I could be a beautiful angel like you one day," Lizzie whispered.

The angel smiled. "Well Lizzie, you have to be very good to become an angel," she replied. "But I'm sure you can do it if you try."

Lizzie nodded.
"Yes, I think I can,"
Lizzie said. "I'll be much nicer from now on."

When Lizzie woke up the next morning, she remembered the angel's visit. "Today I'll be different," she thought. "I'm going to try to be good all day long."

In the morning, Lizzie played with her toys.
She spread them all over the floor, and made a big mess.
"Please put your toys away now, Lizzie," Mom said.
Lizzie was about to shake her head and say that she didn't want to.

But then she remembered
what the angel had told her.
It would be nice if she
could help Mom.
So Lizzie put everything away
neatly in her toy box.
"Thank you, Lizzie," Mom said,
delighted. "What a good girl
you are."

That afternoon, Lizzie's grandma came to visit.
Without being asked, Lizzie ran up to her
and gave her a big kiss.
"Hello, Lizzie!" said Grandma happily.
"It's lovely to see you."

Lizzie and Grandma had a wonderful time.
Lizzie drew Grandma a special picture, which she was very pleased with.
Then they played lots of nice games together.
And everyone enjoyed all the delicious treats Lizzie's Mom had made.

That evening, after Grandma had gone home, Lizzie wanted to play.
"Please play quietly," said Mom. "Matthew's sleeping."
Lizzie wanted to play noisily, and she started to jump across the floor.
But then she remembered what the angel had said.

Matthew hadn't woken up, so Lizzie tiptoed silently across the room and chose a book from the shelf. She sat quietly on a bean bag to look at it. Lizzie didn't make a single sound.

As the days and weeks passed by, Lizzie
was hardly naughty at all.
One day, Mom and Dad had a special
surprise for her.

"We're very proud of you," said Dad,
giving Lizzie a big hug. "You've been
such a good girl lately,
we've gotten a present for you."

Dad handed Lizzie a box.
Inside was a beautiful
silver necklace. There was an
angel charm hanging from it.

"An angel of your own for our little angel," said Mom.
She put the necklace around Lizzie's neck.
"Oh! Thank you, Mom!" beamed Lizzie
as she gave her mom a great big hug.